The Pet Keeper Fairies

For Emelia Macmichael
with lots of love

Special thanks to
Sue Mongredien

ORCHARD BOOKS
338 Euston Road, London NW1 3BH
Orchard Books
Hachette Children's Books
Level 17/207 Kent Street, Sydney, NSW 2000
A Paperback Original

First published in Great Britain in 2006
Rainbow Magic is a registered trademark of Working Partners Limited.
Series created by Working Partners Limited, London W6 OQT

Text © Working Partners Limited 2006
Illustrations © Georgie Ripper 2006
The right of Georgie Ripper to be identified as the illustrator
of this work has been asserted by her in accordance
with the Copyright, Designs and Patents Act, 1988.
A CIP catalogue record for this book is available
from the British Library.

ISBN 1 84616 171 1
1 3 5 7 9 10 8 6 4 2

Printed and bound in China

Penny
the Pony
Fairy

by Daisy Meadows

illustrated by Georgie Ripper

ORCHARD BOOKS

www.rainbowmagic.co.uk

The Fairyland Palace

Wetherbury Village

Strawberry Farm

The Spring Show

Jack Frost's
Ice Castle

Bramble
Stables

Jane Dillon's House

ne Park

Kirsty's
House

Jamie
Cooper's
House

The
Wainwrights'
House

Fairies with their pets I see
And yet no pet has chosen me!
So I will get some of my own
To share my perfect frosty home.

This spell I cast. Its aim is clear:
To bring the magic pets straight here.
Pet Keeper Fairies soon will see
Their seven pets living with me!

Contents

A Pony Ride

"Off we go, Jet!" Kirsty Tate shook the reins and Jet, the handsome black pony she was riding, set off along the forest trail. She grinned over at her friend Rachel Walker who was sitting on a chestnut mare called Annie. The two girls had come for an afternoon's pony ride at

Bramble Stables. "This is the perfect day for riding," Kirsty said happily, feeling the warm sun on her face.

"And the perfect way to end our holiday together," Rachel agreed.

The girls exchanged a secret smile.

Rachel had been staying with Kirsty's family for the whole of the half-term break, and they'd had a very exciting time helping the fairies of Fairyland! Jack Frost had stolen all of the Pet Keeper Fairies' magical pets. This was because, in Fairyland, pets choose their owners themselves, and no pet had ever chosen Jack Frost. In a rage, the naughty fairy had taken the Pet Keeper Fairies' magic pets to his ice castle.

Luckily, the clever pets had managed to escape but they then got lost in the human world. Rachel and Kirsty had spent their half-term holiday rescuing the pets before Jack Frost's sneaky goblin servants could capture them again. So far, the girls had rescued six of the seven missing pets.

"We still need to find Penny the Pony Fairy's pet pony," Kirsty said, thinking aloud. "I really hope we can rescue her before you have to go home, Rachel."

Rachel nodded. "Well, we're definitely in the right place to spot her," she said. "This is pony heaven!"

Bramble Stables was set in a particularly pretty area of countryside, right on the edge of Green Wood forest.

As the horses ambled along the path, the girls could smell the fresh scent of the pine trees in the air, and hear birds calling to one another high in the branches.

One of the stablehands, Jessica, was leading the ride, and behind her rode another little girl and two boys. Kirsty and Rachel were at the rear of the group. They guided their horses next to each other and chatted as they trotted along.

After a few minutes, the trail took the riders past a large pond with a few white geese bobbing serenely on its surface.

"Those are snow geese," Jessica called back to the others. "See their black wing tips?"

Kirsty gazed at the geese as they drifted along on the water. Then, a sudden movement caught her eye. "Look, there's a rabbit," she said, pointing it out as it scuttled behind a bush.

"Oh, and there's a squirrel up there in that tree!" Rachel added. She showed Kirsty where it was perched on a branch, watching the horses go by with its bright eyes.

Suddenly, Kirsty spotted a flash of green disappearing amongst the trees. "What's that?" she murmured to herself, peering through the leaves. But then she gasped. "Oh, Rachel, look," she whispered. "It's a goblin!"

Rachel looked and glimpsed one of Jack Frost's goblins peeping out from behind a tree. Then she saw that there was another one sitting high up on a branch!

"If the goblins are here, they must think Penny's magic pony is somewhere nearby," Rachel said. A determined look came over her face. "And if she is, we've just got to find her before they do!"

Kirsty nodded and the girls rode on, both keeping a close look out for more goblins and the magic pony.

Suddenly, there came several loud bangs that sounded like fireworks. The horses at the front of the group neighed in fright and reared up. Jessica controlled her horse expertly, but the riders behind her panicked as their horses bolted.

Kirsty's horse, Jet, whinnied nervously and broke into a gallop, and Rachel's horse, Annie, followed immediately.

"Try to stay calm!" Jessica shouted to the group. "And hold tight!"

Rachel and Kirsty clung onto their reins as their horses galloped along. "Do you think that noise might have been caused by the goblins?" Rachel called over to Kirsty.

"I don't know," Kirsty called back, "but whatever it was, these horses are well and truly spooked!"

The horses thundered on, and the girls saw that, ahead of them, the trail

forked. The ponies in front swerved down the right-hand trail without breaking their stride, but just as Jet and Annie were approaching the fork, two goblins suddenly popped out from behind some bushes and set off two more loud bangers.

The noise scared Jet and Annie – who promptly bolted down the left-hand trail.

"Oh, no!" Kirsty cried. "Now we're going in the wrong direction!"

Magic in the Meadow

Rachel tried desperately to soothe her frightened mare. "It's all right, Annie," she said. "Don't worry!"

She was speaking as calmly as possible but couldn't help feeling scared herself. The horses were racing along at breakneck speed now, and it was all Rachel could do to keep her balance.

Don't panic! she told herself, sitting right down into the saddle and drawing back steadily on the reins. She glanced across at Kirsty to see her friend doing the same thing and, at last, the horses slowed. Moments later, both girls were able to bring their ponies to a complete stop in a clearing.

"Phew!" Kirsty gasped shakily, sliding off Jet's back. "That was exciting."

"But scary, too," Rachel confessed, slipping down from Annie and giving her a reassuring pat. "Good girl, Annie."

Kirsty gazed around the pretty green
meadow. "I wonder where we are.
Do you think the horses will know the
way back?"

But Rachel was only half listening.
Out of the corner of her eye, she'd
spotted something glittering like fairy
magic on the other
side of the clearing.
"Kirsty, look!" she
said, pointing, but
the glitter vanished
before she had
finished speaking.

Rachel rubbed her eyes and stared
hard, but everything looked perfectly
normal now. "I'm sure I saw something
magical," she told Kirsty, quickly
tying Annie's reins to a nearby tree.

"Let's have a closer look."

Kirsty tethered Jet next to Annie and followed Rachel. Both girls began searching through the undergrowth. Then it was Kirsty's turn to spot something: a glimmer of fairy dust near some rocks!

"Rachel, over here!" she called, crouching down to see where the fairy dust was coming from. And then she smiled. "Oh, Rachel!" she whispered. "Come and see; she's so sweet!"

Rachel knelt down next to Kirsty and smiled too. There, shyly poking her head out from underneath a dandelion, was a tiny, white, sparkling pony. "This must be Penny's magic pony!" Rachel breathed. "And she's really cute!"

"Hello, little pony," Kirsty said in a soft voice, stroking the pony's tiny nose gently with one finger. "Please can you help us? Our horses were scared by Jack Frost's goblins. They ran and ran, and we got separated from our group, and now we're lost."

The magic pony gave a tiny whinny, as if she understood perfectly what Kirsty had said, and trotted towards Jet and Annie. Then, in a flash of fairy magic, she became a full-sized pony with the brightest, whitest coat the girls had ever seen. The pony touched noses with Jet and Annie, and a stream of silvery fairy dust swirled around the three horses. Jet and Annie seemed to calm down at once, and Rachel grinned at Kirsty.

"Fairy pet magic to the rescue once again!" she said happily.

The magic pony whinnied a second time and tossed her head in the direction of a path that led out of the clearing. She trotted a little way towards the path, then turned back and whinnied again.

"She's showing us the way out," Kirsty guessed. "Come on, then, Jet." She untied Jet from the tree, took his reins and gave his glossy black coat a pat. "Are you all right now, boy? Is it OK if I climb up onto your back again?"

Jet nuzzled Kirsty's shoulder and whickered softly. "I'll take that as a yes," Kirsty said, and put her foot into the stirrup.

But before she could haul herself
up into the saddle, Rachel grabbed
Kirsty's arm.

"I can hear voices!" Rachel whispered.

Kirsty stood still, and listened. "You're
right; someone's coming," she hissed.
"It's the goblins! Quick, we must hide!"

Hiding the Horses

Rachel looked around frantically. "Where?" she gulped. The clearing was surrounded by trees, but none of them were big enough to hide the girls and all three horses.

Before Kirsty could reply, both girls heard a silvery voice from behind them exclaim, "Glitter! You're safe!"

PennyPenn

Kirsty and Rachel
turned around
quickly to see
a squirrel scampering
down a nearby
tree, with Penny
the Pony Fairy on
his back! The little
fairy fluttered off the
squirrel's back and thanked
him politely. Then she flew across to
her pony, looking delighted to see her.
Penny had long golden hair that
tumbled over her shoulders. She wore
purple knee-high boots, with jeans
and a pretty purple and white shirt.

"Thank you for finding Glitter," Penny
cried happily, landing on her pony's
nose and kissing her.

"Hello Penny," Kirsty said in a low voice. "Unfortunately, the goblins will find her, too, if we don't get out of sight quickly. They're coming this way!"

"And there's nowhere to hide!" Rachel added. She looked over her shoulder uneasily. The goblins' voices were getting louder and Rachel was sure she could hear their footsteps now. They were sure to spot Glitter at any moment!

Penny quickly waved her wand over the nearest tree. It was a tall oak, but as the silvery fairy dust from Penny's wand swirled around it, the oak became a weeping willow, with long, drooping, leafy branches.

"Brilliant!" Kirsty grinned, leading Jet quickly under the willow tree. "It's the perfect hiding place!"

Rachel led Annie under the tree, too, and Glitter and Penny followed – just in time. The girls held their breath as they heard the goblins coming closer and closer.

"We scared them good and proper with our party poppers!" they heard one goblin boasting. "That magic pony is bound to come now," another of them jeered. "Those magic pets always come to help frightened animals in the human world, don't they?" "Well, let's hope it turns up soon," a third goblin voice said. "This is our last chance to get a pet for Jack Frost, and if it goes wrong again, we're all going to be in big trouble."

35

Very carefully, Kirsty peeped through the willow fronds. She could see some of the goblins were holding party poppers, and one goblin had colourful paper streamers dangling over his big green ears.

"I can't wait to get my hands on that pony, can you?" the first goblin said, grinning.

"It stands no chance with all seven of us after it!" another goblin chuckled.

The goblins started bickering loudly about which goblin would get to ride the magic pony first, and Kirsty, Rachel and Penny exchanged worried glances.

"We have to get Glitter away from here," Rachel whispered to Penny. "Maybe now would be a good time, while they're all arguing?"

Penny nodded. "If you and Kirsty take Jet and Annie, I'll ask Glitter to lead us back to the trail," she said in a tiny fairy whisper.

Kirsty and Rachel quietly swung themselves back into their saddles while Penny fluttered to one of Glitter's ears and whispered into it. Glitter nodded and then, when they were all ready to go, she stepped silently out of the willow tree, away from where the goblins were still arguing.

Rachel held her breath as Annie pushed her nose through the willow fronds, and edged out of the hiding place. Jet followed. The horses were super-quiet. They seemed to know instinctively that they had to be quiet to protect Glitter.

But then, just as Kirsty was thinking that they might escape unheard, Jet trod on a dry twig that snapped with a loud crack!

"What was that?" shouted one of the goblins. "Is somebody there?"

All the goblins turned in the direction of the girls. "Oho! The magic pony – it's right here!" cheered one goblin, hopping from one foot to the other in glee.

"Run, Glitter!" Penny urged fearfully, and Glitter broke into a gallop away from the goblins.

"After them!" bellowed the goblins as one, charging towards the ponies.

"Come on, Jet!" Kirsty said, crouching low over his neck as he and Annie raced after Glitter. The trees were a blur as the horses galloped through the forest, and then on to the trail! Kirsty felt her spirits rise. Surely there was no way the goblins would be able to keep up with the horses at this pace.

"We've lost them!" Rachel cheered after a couple of minutes. "Well done, Annie. We did it!"

"We must be near the end of the trail by now," Kirsty said, as the horses slowed to a trot once more. "We might come out near the stable yard soon."

"Can you imagine Jessica's face if we ride back in there with Glitter, and a horde of goblins?" Rachel laughed in reply.

Kirsty was about to laugh, too, but then she looked ahead and completely forgot about laughing. There, blocking the path – and looking furious – was Jack Frost himself!

An Icy Escape

Kirsty gasped as Jet reared up at the sight of him. Annie neighed in fear too, and backed away.

Jack Frost just gave a horrible cackle and chanted a spell. Immediately, a rope of ice came snaking through the air and looped itself around Glitter's neck.

Jack Frost laughed triumphantly and pulled the pony towards him. "Now I'll have you for my pet!" he declared.

"Oh no!" cried Penny, waving her wand desperately. A stream of silvery fairy dust whirled all around Glitter, and Kirsty and Rachel watched hopefully. But the mighty Jack Frost's magic was clearly too powerful for Penny, and her fairy dust fizzled out uselessly around Glitter's hooves.

"Oh yes," smirked Jack Frost, as he leapt onto Glitter's back. "Your new name is Icicle," he told the little pony. "And you're all mine now. Let's go!"

The girls stared in horror as Jack Frost urged Glitter into a canter and rode away.

"Penny, why don't you ride in my pocket?" Kirsty suggested. "Come on, Rachel, we've got to try and catch up with Glitter!"

The little fairy dived gratefully into Kirsty's shirt pocket. Kirsty could feel her there, quivering with anxiety, as the horses galloped after their new friend.

To Rachel's surprise, they seemed to be gaining on Glitter faster than she'd expected. "I think Glitter's trying to hang back," she said to Kirsty. "I'm sure she's not going as fast as she can!"

The smile was back on Penny's face as she peeped out of Kirsty's pocket. "You're right," she told Rachel. "Clever Glitter – she wants us to catch her up!"

Jack Frost rode right past the sign that pointed back to the stable yard and headed off along the trail. By now the girls' horses were closing in on him steadily. Jack Frost was just about to ride past the pond when he glanced over his shoulder and saw the girls right on his tail.

Stables

With a look of alarm, he grabbed his wand and shouted out a spell. The pond immediately froze over, and Jack Frost guided Glitter towards the ice. "Come on, Icicle!" he urged. "Faster!" Glitter took a few tentative steps across the ice. Then, with a wicked smile, Jack Frost leaned back and waved his wand over the icy stretch she'd just passed. Instantly, that part of the ice melted back to water.

"He's making it impossible for us to follow him across the pond," Kirsty realised in dismay. "We'll have to go around instead."

"But we can't," Rachel said. "There's no path. We'll have to—" She broke off suddenly as a flock of snow geese flew overhead and swooped down towards the far side of the pond.

The girls and Penny watched as the biggest snow goose landed first, not far from Jack Frost and Glitter. The goose pecked at the ice, looking puzzled, and then gave a cross-sounding honk. The other geese honked in annoyance, too, as they realised their pond was frozen.

At the volley of honking, Glitter pricked her ears up and refused to go any nearer to the noisy geese. Jack Frost dismounted and tried to pull her along the ice by his rope, but the little pony stood her ground, and wouldn't take another step.

"Well done, geese! They've stopped Jack Frost in his tracks," Rachel said. Then a thought struck her. "And I've just had a brilliant idea!"

Feathered Friends

"Maybe if Penny turns us into fairies, Kirsty, we could all fly over to the geese," Rachel said, her words tumbling out in excitement. "And if we can somehow get them on our side, they might be able to help us rescue Glitter!"

"Great idea!" Penny said.

Rachel and Kirsty quickly tethered their horses to a nearby tree, then Penny waved her wand again and magicked them both into fairies. "And here's some extra fairy magic so that the geese will understand what you're saying," she said, sprinkling more fairy dust over the girls.

The geese were still making a lot of noise as the three friends flew towards them.

"He did this, you know!" Rachel called out to them, pointing at Jack Frost. "He froze your pond!"

Every goose's head turned in the naughty fairy's direction. The biggest snow goose waggled her tail feathers and honked loudly at the others. Then they all waddled over to Jack Frost in a very business-like way. When they reached him, the geese tapped meaningfully at the ice with their beaks. When Jack Frost ignored them, they began pecking at his legs.

"Hey!" he shouted in surprise. "Stop that!"

But the geese took no notice whatsoever. Soon Jack Frost was surrounded by honking, pecking, angry geese! Glitter didn't seem to like the noisy geese at all. She shied away from them, tugging on her icy rope. Jack Frost was so busy trying to stop the geese pecking him that the rope slipped out of his fingers – and Glitter was free!

Penny flew over to the pony at once, and waved her wand. Fairy dust streamed out, and the rope of ice turned into sparkling snowflakes that floated away and melted on the breeze. Then Glitter shrank to fairy pet size once again.

Penny threw her arms around the little pony. "Oh, Glitter!" Penny cried joyfully. "Thank goodness you're all right!"

The pony neighed softly and nuzzled Penny's hand happily. Penny waved her wand and produced a juicy red apple which she fed to Glitter. Kirsty smiled to see Glitter and Penny reunited. Then she turned to see if Jack Frost had noticed. He was still trying to get away from the geese, but as he pushed the biggest goose away with his hand, beautiful, magical sparkles glittered around the goose and Jack Frost.

"What's that? What's happening?" Kirsty asked Penny.

Penny chuckled. "A pet has finally chosen Jack Frost as its owner!" she explained with a grin. "The snow goose wants to be Jack Frost's pet!"

"Or does she want him to be her pet?" Kirsty giggled.

On the other side of the pond, Jack Frost's goblins came crashing through the trees, but they were too late to help their master now.

Jack Frost's gaze fell upon Glitter, safe with Penny, and he held up his hands in defeat. "All right! I'll turn the ice back to water," he cried in desperation. "As long as you geese leave me alone and stop that awful racket!" He stalked off the pond and waved his wand. The ice instantly melted away, and with a satisfied wiggling of tail feathers, the geese turned and waddled back to the pond, launching themselves into the water, one by one.

"Come on," Jack Frost called to the goblins, grumpily. "Let's go home."

The goblins trailed after their master as he stomped towards the trees.

Suddenly, with a honk of surprise, the biggest snow goose flew after them, landed by Jack Frost's side, and pushed her beak affectionately into his hand.

"Ahh, she doesn't want him to leave without her," Penny said, smiling.

"How sweet!" Kirsty exclaimed, as the goose gazed lovingly at her new owner. The other geese came out of the water, too, waddling over to join Jack Frost and the goblins.

"It's nice to have a pet," Penny agreed, patting Glitter. "I'm glad Jack Frost has got someone to love now, too. And I'm even more glad I've got Glitter back," she added, smiling at Kirsty and Rachel. "Thanks so much, girls!"

Rachel fluttered her wings happily. "Now all of the fairy pets are safe," she beamed. "We did it!"

"I'd better take Glitter back to Fairyland," Penny went on. "Would you two like to come with me?"

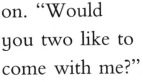

A smile broke over Kirsty's face. "Yes, please," she cried eagerly, but then she looked over to where Jet and Annie were tethered. "But we should really get the horses back to the stable," she said.

"The horses will be fine," Penny said reassuringly. "I'll work some magic so that it seems as if you're only away from them for a second."

"Hurrah!" Rachel cheered. "Then we'd love to come to Fairyland!"

Perfect Pets for Everyone

Penny waved her wand and a cloud
of fairy dust billowed from the tip,
enveloping herself, the girls and Glitter
in a whirl of sparkles. Seconds later,
the girls found themselves in Fairyland,
right outside the palace.

King Oberon and Queen Titania
were waiting in the palace gardens,

along with all the other Pet Keeper Fairies.

"Welcome back, Kirsty and Rachel," the Queen said, smiling at them. "Thank you so much for helping our Pet Keeper Fairies."

The King stepped forwards. "You did well, my dears. Once again, you have helped the fairies beyond measure."

Rachel and Kirsty curtseyed. "It was a pleasure, Your Majesties," Kirsty said politely.

"But what if Jack Frost tries to steal our pets again?" Bella the Bunny Fairy asked. "How do we know they'll be safe?"

Penny gave her a wink. "Don't worry, Bella," she said. "Now that Jack Frost has his very own pet, he doesn't need to steal anybody else's."

The Queen smiled and sprinkled a little fairy dust over the garden's pond. The surface shimmered with magic, and Kirsty and Rachel leaned over to look as a picture appeared. It showed Jack Frost's palace – with a new pond in front of it!

"That wasn't there before," Kirsty said with a grin.

"And look! There are the geese!" Rachel laughed. "They look very content in their new home, don't they?"

The girls smiled to see Jack Frost sitting on a bench near his pond, feeding the largest snow goose with some bread, and patting her gently. The two really did seem fond of each other.

Katie the Kitten Fairy cuddled Shimmer, her kitten. "The fairy pets are definitely safe now," she said. "Hurrah!"

Sunny the puppy bounded over to Rachel just then, and gave her a lick as if to say thank you. Then Sparky the guinea pig squeaked something.

"She says, 'Well done, Kirsty and Rachel'," Georgia translated with a grin.

"I think we all agree with Sparky," the Queen said, with a little smile at the excited guinea pig. "But I'm afraid I must return you to your own world now, girls. Annie and Jet need you to take them back to the stable yard."

"They know the way," the King added. "You'll find Jessica and the others waiting there. If you hurry, you'll get back before Jessica has to ride out looking for you."

"Before you go, though, we'd like you each to have one of these," the Queen said. She waved her wand, filling the air with a flurry of golden fairy dust. When the dust cleared, Kirsty and Rachel saw that they each had a new charm bracelet sparkling on their wrists. The bracelets were made of

a silver chain, and were hung with
seven tiny charms that shimmered with
all the colours of the rainbow.

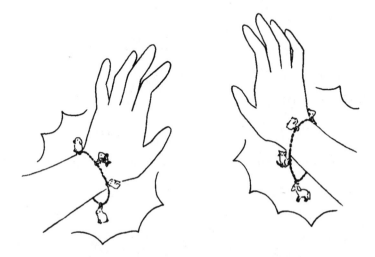

"Oh, Kirsty, look!" Rachel cried in
delight. "A kitten, a rabbit, a hamster,
a guinea pig, a puppy, a goldfish and
a pony!"

"You'll never forget your adventures
with the Pet Keeper Fairies now," the
King told them, his eyes twinkling.

Kirsty shook her head. "Never ever," she agreed. "Thank you so much. And goodbye, all of you. I hope we'll see you again soon!"

"Goodbye," Rachel said. "Thanks for the bracelets. I've really enjoyed our adventures."

"Goodbye," the Pet Keeper Fairies chorused, running over to hug the girls one last time.

Then the Queen raised her wand and waved it over the girls. The world seemed to spin in a blizzard of fairy dust, and then Rachel and Kirsty found  themselves back by the ponies.

Kirsty untied Jet and swung herself up onto his back. "Let's get back to the stable yard like the King told us," she said. "With a bit of luck, we'll still have time to go out with Jessica for one last ride before my mum comes to collect us."

"Good idea," Rachel said, climbing up onto Annie. Then she grinned at Kirsty. "Race you there!"

Win a Rainbow Magic
Sparkly T-Shirt and Goody Bag!

In every book in the Rainbow Magic Pet Keeper Fairies series (books 29-35) there is a hidden picture of a collar with a secret letter in it. Find all seven letters and re-arrange them to make a special Fairyland word, then send it to us. Each month we will put the entries into a draw and select one winner to receive a Rainbow Magic Sparkly T-shirt and Goody Bag!

Send your entry on a postcard to Rainbow Magic Pet Keeper Competition, Orchard Books, 338 Euston Road, London NW1 3BH. Australian readers should write to Hachette Children's Books, Level 17/207 Kent Street, Sydney, NSW 2000.
Don't forget to include your name and address.
Only one entry per child. Final draw: 30th April 2007.

Don't miss...
Kylie the Carnival Fairy

1-84616-175-4

Kylie the Carnival Fairy needs Kirsty's and Rachel's help! Jack Frost has stolen the three magic hats that make the Sunnydays Carnival so much fun, and the girls have to get them back...

Have you checked out the

website at:

www.rainbowmagic.co.uk

There are games, activities and fun things to do, as well as news and information about Rainbow Magic and all of the fairies.

by Daisy Meadows

The Jewel Fairies

The Pet Keeper Fairies

All priced at £3.99. *Holly the Christmas Fairy, Summer the Holiday Fairy,*
Stella the Star Fairy and *Kylie the Carnival Fairy* are priced at £4.99.
The Rainbow Magic Treasury is priced at £12.99.
Rainbow Magic books are available from all good bookshops, or can be ordered
direct from the publisher: Orchard Books, PO BOX 29, Douglas IM99 1BQ
Credit card orders please telephone 01624 836000
or fax 01624 837033 or visit our Internet site: www.wattspub.co.uk
or e-mail: bookshop@enterprise.net for details.

To order please quote title, author and ISBN and your full name and address.
Cheques and postal orders should be made payable to 'Bookpost plc.'
Postage and packing is FREE within the UK
(overseas customers should add £2.00 per book).
Prices and availability are subject to change.

Look out for the Fun Day Fairies!

MEGAN THE MONDAY FAIRY
1-84616-188-6

TALLULAH THE TUESDAY FAIRY   1-84616-189-4

WILLOW THE WEDNESDAY FAIRY   1-84616-190-8

THEA THE THURSDAY FAIRY   1-84616-191-6

FREYA THE FRIDAY FAIRY
1-84616-192-4

SIENNA THE SATURDAY FAIRY
1-84616-193-2

SARAH THE SUNDAY FAIRY
1-84616-194-0

Available from
Saturday 2nd September 2006